W9-ASR-807

The Sky Is Falling

The Sky Is Falling!

For my daughter Kiera,
who is just learning to read—CF

First Aladdin Paperbacks Edition April 1998

Aladdin Paperbacks
An imprint of Simon & Schuster Children's Publishing Division
1230 Avenue of the Americas
New York, NY 10020

The text for this book was set in Utopia.
Printed and bound in the United States of America
10 9 8 7 6 5 4

The Library of Congress has cataloged the Simon & Schuster
Books for Young Readers Edition as follows:
Miles, Betty
The sky is falling / by Betty Miles ; illustrated by Cynthia Fisher.
p. cm. — (Ready-to-read)
Summary: A retelling of the cumulative folktale in which a silly chicken and
her barnyard friends run around shouting that the sky is falling.
ISBN 0-689-81791-6 (pbk.)
[1. Folklore.] I. Fisher, Cynthia, ill. II. Chicken Licken. III. Title. IV. Series.
PZ8.1.M5995Sk 1998
398.2—dc21
[E] 97-17351
CIP   AC

The Sky Is Falling!

WRITTEN BY
Betty Miles

ILLUSTRATED BY
Cynthia Fisher

Ready-to-Read
Aladdin Paperbacks

OLD STORIES FOR NEW READERS

The Sky Is Falling! is an old story, and old stories are good for new readers. When they know what is going to happen, it's easier for them to read the words that tell about it.

Old stories often use the same words, like "Help, help! The sky is falling!" over and over again. A new reader begins to expect those words, to enjoy them, and to learn them.

And rhyming words help new readers. The names in this story, like Chicken Licken and Foxy Loxy, are fun to say and easy to read.

You give your new reader a good start when you read out loud to each other. In this book, all the words are the animals' talk. Your child can read one animal's words and you can read another's.

Take time to enjoy the story and the pictures. You can help your reader by talking about what is happening on the page and what might happen next. You can point to familiar words in the pictures and to words that rhyme. You can help by asking what sound a word begins with.

Most of all, you can help by reading together often. Your new reader can read with you or with a grandparent, a babysitter, an older brother, sister, or a friend. New readers love to share their books!

OW!

Oh, my goodness.
The sky is falling!

7

Help, help,
Henny Penny.
The sky is falling!

Oh, my goodness!
The sky is falling!

Help, Ducky Lucky!
The sky is falling!
Chicken Licken says so!

Oh, my goodness!
The sky is falling!
The sky is falling!

Help, Turkey Lurkey!
The sky is falling!
Chicken Licken
and Henny Penny say so!

13

Oh, my goodness!
Help!

Bonk!

Help, help, Goosey Loosey!
The sky is falling!
Chicken Licken, Ducky Lucky,
and Henny Penny say so!

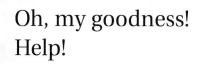

Oh, my goodness!
Help!

Help, help, Foxy Loxy!
The sky is falling!